KALEIDOSCOPE

KALEIDOSCOPE

Written by

Alan R. Paine, Angela Caulder, Annie Percik, Claire Wilson, Erin English, Ian Coldicott, Jack Mann, John Kot, Kester Park, Madeleine McDonald, Mark P. Henderson, Sue Knight, Vanessa Horn, & Walt Pilcher

First Published in 2023 by Fantastic Books Publishing
Cover image by Bea Burchill
Cover design by Gabi

ISBN (ebook): 978-1-914-060-48-9
ISBN (paperback): 978-1-914-060-47-2

This collection is dedicated to the memory of
Neil 'Boff' Boffin, a cherished and much missed member of
the Elite Dangerous community and beyond,
taken from us far too soon. Fly safe, Commander.

Acknowledgements

This anthology has been supported and sponsored by two amazing charities; **Special Effect** who put fun and inclusion back into the lives of physically disabled people across the world; and **Stack Up** who promote positive mental health and combat veteran suicide through gaming and geek culture.

Special Effect transforms the lives of people with physical challenges right across the world through the innovative use of technology. At the core of their mission is their work to optimise inclusion, enjoyment and quality of life by helping people control video games to the best of their abilities. Special Effect's team of occupational therapists and gaming specialists in the UK create bespoke control setups for hundreds of individuals each year, while their R&D team use what they learn in the field to develop freely-available resources and solutions to help level the playing field for gamers with physical challenges all over the world.

This mission of inclusion extends beyond gaming, whether by using eye-gaze technology to bring communication, independence and hope for people in intensive care units with a severe injury or illness, or by using telepresent robots to reconnect medically isolated children with their education and friends.

Stack Up supports military veterans with its four pillar programs:

* Supply Crates are video game care packages full of the latest games, gear, and consoles sent to deployed units and veterans in need.
* Air Assaults are all-expenses-paid trips to bring deserving veterans to gaming and geek culture events.
* The Stacks are volunteer teams engaged in veteran outreach and community betterment projects in their local areas.
* Overwatch Program is 24/7 crisis intervention and peer-to-peer mental health support for veterans and civilians alike, provided through Stack Up's online community.

With thanks also to those who supported these charities by entering the competition and congratulations to the winners and the shortlisted authors whose stories are published in this anthology.

Contents

Thug *by Angela Caulder*

Steve finished watering the pansies and stood back to admire his work. The front garden looked neat and fresh now. He walked to the shed in the back garden to put away the tools, carefully cleaning them to a pristine shine so his Aunt didn't get annoyed. She always seemed annoyed these days; he tried to minimise it as much as possible. He hated her shouting. Earlier he'd baked her favourite lemon cake before putting in his shift at the foodbank outside Sainsbury's. He had handed in his supermarket application and was waiting on the manager getting back to him about an interview. Fingers crossed. He needed the cash.

After his shower he clumped down the stairs thinking about his meagre savings. He was determined to keep them growing, there were so many important things he needed to do. Petronella, his Aunt's dog was waiting for him at the bottom of the stairs. The whole of her small body wiggled from side to side as she wagged her tail to greet him. He attached her lead and she led him out for their twice daily walk. The mask was on as the new variant was apparently prevalent in South Norwood.

He pondered as they walked at how Covid had changed his life. When the virus hit, his arrogance had been as large as his flabby body. Both had changed since. Petronella yapped aggressively at a rather nervous Rhodesian Ridgeback that shot past them bringing Steve back to the present. He thought himself lucky. His Aunt took him in and was okay about the free weights in the conservatory as long as he did the gardening. He'd grown to love the garden; his flabbiness had diminished and he'd stayed away from his old haunts.

Walking Petronella in his mask had produced some unexpected results. People talked to him. No, not only talked, they chatted and smiled. Ordinary people with ordinary conversation, and he was one of them and he liked it! The mask hid The Thug. No-one would have stopped to talk to The Thug.

Coming out of the park onto the empty high street, he stopped in front of a shop window with a large bejewelled mirror in the centre. He pulled his mask down and looked long and gloomily at his face. The Thug had been put away for ABH, getting away with GBH by a whisker. The Thug didn't really have good mates, just a one-upmanship on who could be the most violent, the best with the ladies, the one with the coolest stuff. It was all shit really. Pentonville taught him that. He would grow his savings. The word 'Thug', tattooed in blue, at the bottom of his left cheek was no longer wanted.

About the author
Angela Caulder has worked in public service for over 30 years as an NHS Manager, Dramatherapist and Children's Social Worker. She writes for pleasure when she cannot resist the urge and has time. She lives in South West London, and loves the time spent with two talented daughters who are at Uni, who bring her inspiration and joy. She hopes readers will enjoy the humour of the story juxtaposed with the more serious themes of difference and possibilities for change.

Thug was the joint 1st prize-winner in the competition.

It's a Frog Eat Frog World *by Alan R Paine*

Goran Oudermans was one of the few historians who dared to delve into the dark ages of Martian history. The video file that he had found appeared to date from just after the time that Earth cut off all assistance to the fledgling colony; a period that most people didn't want to be reminded of.

'Ladies and gentlemen,' said a voice off camera, 'We are proud to present the one woman on Mars who's more fun standing up than lying down, your very own Sunny Sutton.' Applause.

'Thank you, thank you. Yes, that's right, my name's Sunny – like the weather. Do any of you get out much? You know I went for a walk outside once and, tell you what, the beach is amazing but the tide goes out a hell of a long way. What's that? The sea dried up a billion years ago? Trust me to be late for the fun. But it doesn't really matter because I've got nothing to wear for the beach. I was going to bring a chiffon bikini from Earth but I couldn't afford the excess baggage fee.

'But I still managed to fool them at the pre-flight weigh in. I breathed out and saved $1000.' The audience found this particularly funny.

'Seriously now, it's amazing how things are done here. See this glass of wine, only yesterday this was someone's pee.' She took a sip. 'No, sorry I was wrong, it still is someone's pee.'

'And what about this super nutritious algae, ay? You know what that stuff grows on don't you? Yeah, and it tastes like it too. The government could solve the food shortage by encouraging people to go the toilet more often to grow more of the stuff. That would be good, because I always find it a bit embarrassing to say, 'Oh I'm just off for a crap.' In future I'd be able to claim that I was doing my civic duty.'

The audience were clearly enjoying the show but then the mood changed and the laughter became more nervous and restrained.

'I was watching a video the other day about frogs that live in the deserts on Earth. Whenever it rains, they lay their eggs in pools of water and plant eating tadpoles quickly hatch out. But if the pond starts to dry up some of the tadpoles turn carnivorous and chow down on their siblings so that they can reach adulthood before the water's gone. Sound familiar?'

'I don't have to tell you what those jokers at Toad Hall are up to, do I? It's frog eat frog out there. Who's next to be 'randomly' selected for the chop we ask ourselves? Who's going to be chops? If I haven't gone down well tonight maybe I'll be going down well next week. I'm Sunny and you've been a wonderful audience. Goodnight.'

The picture froze and a caption appeared below the image of the smiling young woman. 'In Loving Memory of Sunny 2150 – 2175.'

About the author

Stories by Alan R Paine have been published in five Fantastic Books competition collections: *Dread Cold, Dreaming of Steam, The Forge, The Dummies Guide to Serial Killing,* and now *Kaleidoscope*. His story 'Trains of Thought' in *Dreaming of Steam*, won the Julia Bradbury prize for capturing the spirit of the Wolds.

He collaborated with Drew Wagar and seven other writers

to produce the science fiction anthology 'Nine Streams of Consciousness,' and he has published the short novel 'Faraway Sky, Ocean Deep' which was written, from beginning to end, in the month of November 2020 in response to the challenge set by nanowrimo.org.

Alan's debut full-length Sci-Fi novel, *A Suggestion in Space*, was launched at the same time as this anthology.

Alan enjoys amateur theatre and has written and directed short plays and sketches including a play performed online during lockdown.

It's a Frog Eat Frog World was the joint 1st prize-winner in the competition.

Passing Ships *by Mark P Henderson*

His right hand clasped the air where the dream had been. His fingers caressed the curve of the cumulus, white as a bridal veil, sliding towards the horizon like a ghost ship, drifting and dissolving like the dream he'd dreamed.

Her left hand stretched towards a passing cloud and a sunbeam twined in delight around her third finger. Then the cloud covered the sun. The light faded like a dream, like a ship passing below the horizon.

Later, he married. He was faithful and treated his wife with kindness. He was sure she was not unhappy. But when he awoke his children in the morning or laid them down to sleep at night, they were strangers. Strange: he told bedtime stories to them, but not the story he dared not tell, the tale of a ship that had sailed without him, of a cumulus fragmenting under his fingers.

She never married. She grew older. Day after day she watched clouds caressing her hand, light trickling between her fingers. She became a stranger to those who'd been family and friends, and they thought her strange. They knew there was a story locked in her head, the story of a ship that had awaited her but she hadn't boarded. They never heard the tale. Her wrinkled lips kept it captive.

His right hand reached through the air towards the clouds. She held her left hand to the sky and sought a sunbeam. They watched their disparate dreams dwindle like sinking ships.

About the author

After a career in medicine and university teaching, Mark P. Henderson retired to North Derbyshire in 2002 and started to write fiction, edit manuscripts, teach creative writing, and collect and tell Peak District folktales.

His publications, through five different publishing houses, comprise an anthology of short stories (*Rope Trick,* 2008), a children's story *(Fenella and the Magic Mirror,* 2009), a study of the evolution of a local legend (*Murders in the Winnats Pass,* 2010), a collection of 62 traditional stories (*Folktales of the Peak District,* 2011), a collection of puns in verse and prose (*Cruel and Unusual PunNishments,* 2016), a one-act play (*Forget it, it's History,* 2017), four more novels (*National Cake Day in Ruritania,* 2018; *The Engklimastat,* 2019; *Perilaus II,* 2021, and its sequel, *Con,* 2022), a novelette (*The Definitive Biography of St Arborius of Glossopdale and his Thin Dog,* 2019), and a novella (*The Cat of Doom,* 2020).

His novel about Glossopdale's *real* sixteenth century folk hero, *Black Harry,* was also released in 2022-3.

Elusive Tales of the Peak District, Mark's compilation of folktales from South West Peak was published at the same time as this anthology.

See http://www.peakinthepast.co.uk/folktales.html for the bumpy journey of its development as its author wrestled with the problems of the coronavirus pandemic and a drone camera.

For further details see

http://www.markphenderson.com/

or https://www.amazon.co.uk/Mark-P.-Henderson

Passing Ships was joint runner-up in the competition.

The Rose Garden *by Madeleine McDonald*

"Mrs Palmer, Mrs Palmer, are you alright? Do you want a glass of water?"

I stared down at my knees, and composed my expression. When I raised my head, I saw concern on the estate agent's face. So much the better, I could haggle the price down.

"I'm OK. It was unexpected, that's all."

"We have to be sure customers have a genuine interest in the property before we tell them…" She trailed off.

I made reassuring noises. The information that the previous owner's body was buried in the garden did not account for the shivers of anticipation down my spine.

I knew the house inside out. It was a Victorian mansion, set in a large garden. Darius and I had played in all the rooms as children, and the dusty attic was one of our favourite hiding places.

The agent shuffled her papers and became businesslike again. "It is unusual for someone to be buried on their own property. But I can assure you it is legal. If you are still interested, I'll arrange a viewing."

Darius's parents had been refugees from Iran. They belonged to some tiny, persecuted sect that valued spiritual rewards over earthly concerns. His mother was a mediocre cook who let food burn in the oven when she was listening to music. Or when she was in the garden talking to the roses.

The rose garden, planted by some previous owner, was her sanctuary.

Sitting in the estate agent's office, I recalled a blur of colour and fragrance and wondered what it looked like now.

Darius's parents had money, but were indifferent to material possessions. Beyond repairing the leaky roof, they did nothing to the house, and in so doing preserved the high ceilings and imposing fireplaces.

Once we grew out of eating cake with burnt edges, I began to imagine how I would redecorate the house when it became mine. For I never doubted that Darius and I would marry.

He loved his parents, but an English education had left him agnostic, and he appreciated comfort. My younger self foresaw no obstacles to me restoring our home to its former glory. He would be proud of me.

The drawing room was always the focal point whenever I visualised our future together. Its large French windows would need heavy curtains to keep out the cold in winter, but carefully chosen chintz fabric would echo the delights of the rose garden beyond the terrace.

*

On the first morning in my new home, I take a cup of tea out to the rose garden. I sit on the wooden bench, triumphant in my possession.

The tea cools, and I tip the dregs onto the grass beside Darius's grave.

He did me wrong, marrying someone else. However, she did little to the house and, all these years later, here we are. Together, at home.

I will sit here every day to update him on my projects.

9

About the author

Madeleine McDonald lives in Yorkshire and finds inspiration walking on the empty beach. Her published writing ranges from Shakespearean sonnets to personal reportage. Her historical novel, *A Shackled Inheritance,* is available on Amazon.

The Rose Garden was shortlisted in the competition.

Wormhole *by Walt Pilcher*

15-Year-Old Survives Freak Fall
Billy Bradley, 15, was taken to Mercy Hospital with non-life-threatening injuries Saturday afternoon after apparently jumping from his second story bedroom window into the back yard of his home on Cedar Street. Police and EMTs were dispatched following a 911 call from his parents. Authorities were at a loss to explain why he was found 100 feet from the house. "Billy says he fell, but there's no way he could have fallen or jumped that far out," said his father, Vernon Bradley, "and we don't understand why he seems to look younger." An investigation is continuing.

When the wormhole showed up in Billy Bradley's bedroom, he didn't know what it was. There was no sign saying, "Wormhole," no label from the Acme Wormhole Company saying, "Do not remove under penalty of law," no Surgeon General's warning that wormholes may be hazardous to your health.

As wormholes go, it was a small one. You could ride a bicycle through it, but certainly not a spaceship. Which is why Billy didn't identify it right away even though he had read far more science-fiction than anyone else in his 10th grade class at Carl Sagan High School. To Billy, it simply looked like an amorphous darkish cloud, roughly circular, that was obscuring the view from his desk to his bed on the other side of the room. He could see the bed vaguely, and then he couldn't, and then he could again—it kept winking in and out—as if something inside the cloud was pulsing like a spastic iris, opening and closing, but slowly and erratically.

Billy watched, mesmerized, while he tried to puzzle out what the thing might be. For some reason, he wasn't frightened, only curious. Was it possible? He tossed a much-chewed-on pencil toward it, aiming for the barely visible bed. Never reaching the bed, the pencil hung suspended in mid-air—or mid-thing—for an instant and then disappeared. Where did it go?

He approached the apparition as closely as he dared and heard a faint humming sound, also slightly pulsating, almost like the drone of traffic on a distant highway. No horns or sirens though, just the hum. He stepped back, noticing then that the thing had moved. Not very much, only about as far as the shadow on the floor made by his desk as an afternoon sunbeam traversed the room. But it *was* moving, toward the window. Billy figured it would be through the window and suspended outside, one story above the backyard, in less than an hour.

It was now or never. He climbed into the cloud, hung suspended for a moment, and vanished.

Three hours later, an unblemished pencil came back. Three minutes after that, so did 10-year-old Billy.

About the author
Walt Pilcher lives in Greensboro, NC (USA), with his wife, Carol, an artist. During his apparel industry career he moonlighted as a fiction writer, later adding poetry and song writing with pieces appearing in a range of publications. He divides his time between family (six grandchildren), church, writing, golf and learning guitar.

His debut novel, *Everybody Shrugged*, established him as a writer with a unique ability to weave sublime parody into humour and suspense. He then took these talents and embarked on his Mark Fairley, reluctant Private Eye, series; *The Accidental Spurrt* takes a pop at the fizzy drinks industry; *Killing O'Carolan* parodies the creative industries in ways only Walt can achieve.

His works have also appeared in previous anthologies from Fantastic Books Publishing, Fresh Magazine, the Love, Life and Peace anthology by Stephanie Thomas, and Fire & Chocolate, the 2012 poetry anthology of the Writers' Group of the Triad.

Wormhole was awarded joint 3rd place in the competition.

The Road Less Travelled *by Alan R Paine*

Wherever you travel there are sights that guide books and/or the local tourist board reckon that you have to see. It's great to go to these places but don't forget that you can also look out for things, never mentioned in the guide books, that you can make your own special experience. By all means join the crowds to wonder at the Mona Lisa but don't forget to look behind you to see the magnificent 'Wedding at Cana' by Veronesi.

One of the standard things to see in Crete is the Samaria Gorge, up to 1000 metres deep and at the narrowest point spannable by two people holding hands. It attracts a steady stream of tourists walking through from the top down to the sea. But with a small child in tow, we were going to take the easier option of walking from the coast to the narrowest section and back. We needed to get a bus from a village a few kilometres from where we were staying but rather than take a connecting bus along the main road, we decided to walk along the little country byway between the two places.

Our first reward was a piece of industrial archaeology next to the road. A rusting bucket elevator stood in a well with a concrete circle beside it. At one time a donkey would have walked around driving the conveyor to bring a near continuous stream of water to the surface in rising buckets, that passed over the upper gearwheel, turning upside down and discharging their loads into a channel.

Only a little further on, we spotted a white painted stone

14

chapel hardly bigger than a garden shed. It was locked and when we tried to look in through the tiny window in the door it was too dark to see anything. This was the 1980s and we didn't have a mobile phone with a light and camera on it or anything like that, because they hadn't been invented, so all we could do was get out our film camera, turn on the flash, hold it up to the window and hope for the best.

Weeks later when we got the film back from the processors, we had a wonderful surprise. The little room was full of icons and gold ornaments perfectly captured by the camera's old-fashioned technology. Using modern technology, I have retraced the route using Street View. There's a little chapel in just about the right place but there are so many like it in Greece it's hard to be sure. I couldn't see the bucket elevator at all. Maybe it doesn't exist any more or it's hidden in the bushes. I'll have to go back and take a look but with any luck I'll take a wrong turn and discover something else.

About the author

Stories by Alan R Paine have been published in five Fantastic Books competition collections: *Dread Cold*, *Dreaming of Steam*, *The Forge*, *The Dummies Guide to Serial Killing*, and now *Kaleidoscope*. His story 'Trains of Thought' in *Dreaming of Steam*, won the Julia Bradbury prize for capturing the spirit of the Wolds.

He collaborated with Drew Wagar and seven other writers to produce the science fiction anthology 'Nine Streams of Consciousness,' and he has published the short novel 'Faraway Sky, Ocean Deep' which was written, from beginning to end, in the month of November 2020 in response to the challenge set by nanowrimo.org.

Alan's debut full-length Sci-Fi novel, A Suggestion in Space, was launched at the same time as this anthology.

Alan enjoys amateur theatre and has written and directed short plays and sketches including a play performed on line during lockdown.

The Road Less Travelled was shortlisted in the competition.

The Unspoken *by Vanessa Horn*

I didn't call it bullying when I was younger. I wasn't even aware that it was abnormal behaviour; I just assumed that was how mums and dads behaved with each other. It was only when I reached school age, when I was going off for tea with other kids and seeing what other families were like – well, that's the point at which I started to realise that my parents were different.

I said nothing. I couldn't – I didn't have the words then. Or later. No, I retreated into my own private world, reading and drawing alone in my room. That sort of thing. But I watched when no-one knew I was watching. Listened when no-one knew I was listening. Wondered. And fretted. It wasn't right, surely? Married people were supposed to love each other. Weren't they?

As the years passed, it got worse. It wasn't just the sarcasm anymore, though that was still bad enough. No, now the slaps took over when words petered out. An unexpected adjustment. Random.

Try as I might, I couldn't understand the reason behind it all. If I had, I might have been able to warn, to pre-empt, or maybe even prevent. Maybe. But there was nothing logical about these incidents. They arose, on the face of it, out of nothing.

It seemed beyond explanation. I could only think that perhaps there was some mysterious adulthood code of behaviour I would only understand when I too was grown-up. So, until then, I could only wait. Worry.

It wasn't as if the bruises were exposed. No, they were easy enough to conceal – never on the face or anyplace that couldn't be covered with long sleeves or high necklines. But I knew they were there; I was aware of every slight wince and flinch. I experienced the pain too, in a kind of empathy, I suppose. I still couldn't talk about it though – could only convey my compassion in actions, ineffectual as they seem now. I would fetch a cup of tea, run a bubble bath, that sort of thing. Maybe it made a difference, however small. I hoped it did.

Then there came a day when I was taller than both of them. A day when I wasn't upstairs, quailing at every blow, every strike. No. I was walking into the kitchen to face them – both of them. I was opening my mouth and speaking.

A moment's silence. He looked down, emotions veiled. She looked at me. I couldn't read the expression in her eyes. Shock? Embarrassment? Shame? It didn't matter – all that was important was that she knew I knew. Now she would stop. She had to. For I had found my voice.

About the author

Vanessa Horn is a Junior School teacher who first became interested in writing in 2013, when she took a sabbatical year off from work. Since then, she has written several hundred stories, many of which have been published in magazines, and others having won prizes in short story and flash fiction competitions. In 2015, her first book – a collection of short stories – was published by Alfie Dog Fiction.

Since venturing into writing for children seven years ago, Vanessa's first picture book – Waaaaa! – was released in January 2020 by Tiny Tree Publishing. Later that year, her

THE UNSPOKEN BY VANESSA HORN

collection of flash fiction for adults – Theme and Variations – was published by Chapeltown Books. This is a compilation of stories all based on or around the theme of music.

In her spare time, Vanessa enjoys watercolour painting, playing the piano, and reading.

Twitter handle: @VanessaHorn7

The Unspoken was shortlisted in the competition.

How Now? *By Walt Pilcher*

See, then was now then
and will be then again.
What has been is still;
what's to come has all been.

If then was just now
though they don't share a name
and their meanings seem different,
aren't they yet still the same?

Does Pluto have time zones?
Is it evening on Mars?
Ah, show me the sunsets
of billions of stars.

What time is it now?
Is it now where you are?
Is it now but not now
when light travels so far?

While we've not created
this temporal state,
if we're always in time,
then we cannot be late.

We live in the present,
and while it seems odd,
it's good to have something
in common with God.

About the author

Walt Pilcher lives in Greensboro, NC (USA), with his wife, Carol, an artist. During his apparel industry career he moonlighted as a fiction writer, later adding poetry and song writing with pieces appearing in a range of publications. He divides his time between family (six grandchildren), church, writing, golf and learning guitar.

His debut novel, *Everybody Shrugged*, established him as a writer with a unique ability to weave sublime parody into humour and suspense. He then took these talents and embarked on his Mark Fairley, reluctant Private Eye, series; the first of which, *The Accidental Spurrt*, takes a pop at the fizzy drinks industry; and the second, *Killing O'Carolan* parodies the creative industries in ways only Walt can achieve.

His works have also appeared in previous anthologies from Fantastic Books, Fresh Magazine, the Love, Life and Peace anthology by Stephanie Thomas, and Fire & Chocolate, the 2012 poetry anthology of the Writers' Group of the Triad.

How Now? was shortlisted in the competition.

Talky Tin *by Sue Knight*

Talky Tin sat in the window seat looking inscrutable.

At least that's how everyone said he looked. And then they said what mysterious creatures cats are.

But, although she had tried very hard to see what was inscrutable about him, Emily hadn't been able to so far.

To her, he seemed very easy to read.

When he was happy he purred and smiled. When he was hungry, he wailed and bellowed.

When he was sleepy, he fell asleep. He fell asleep on the instant, wherever he was. Emily had found him slumped by his food bowl; upside down in the flower bed; snoring happily under the feeder while the birds pecked around him.

He loved people, climbing and purring over all visitors. Falling asleep on them if he was sleepy. Wailing at them if he was hungry.

Apparently, to be true to his inscrutable type, he should only have sat on those visitors who were allergic to cats. But everyone was an acceptable cat couch to Talky.

He detested all cats.

And he was not at all inscrutable about making that known. He didn't even bother to go through the elaborate fight rituals of his kind. He fired no warning shots across the bows. Any cat coming within the invisible line Talky had drawn around the property met a business like set of claws and teeth instantly.

They left quickly. And didn't come back.

All in all, Emily thought that Talky was probably from another planet. And he hadn't bothered to do his homework properly. Or perhaps he was just very lazy about his camouflage.

Yet no-one had noticed.

No-one, apart from her. And apparently she didn't matter.

Which left a nagging worry in her mind. If Talky knew that she didn't matter, did that mean that he had spotted her?

About the author

Sue Knight wrote this short story in her expat years, inspired by her lovely, fierce Arabian cat, and by her feeling of being an alien in the world of expats. Sue has had two novels published: *Waiting for Gordo*, and *Disraeli Hall*. Her short story anthology, *The Umbrellas of Hamelin*, was launched at the same time as this anthology. Sue publishes a blog regularly at https://sueknight2000.blogspot.com/

Talky Tin came joint 4th in the competition.

Greener Pastures *by Claire Wilson*

Familiarity breeds contempt.

Those three words rattled around Karen's head like the ball in a pinball game. She'd been employed within the Procurement Department for just a few weeks; however, she despised the location, the measly pay and most importantly, her new boss, Patricia Lawson.

As she stood in the small kitchen being lectured by Patricia on the importance of using the photocopier instead of the printer, Karen felt close to breaking point. Nothing she did was good enough for this woman.

Yesterday she'd been on the receiving end of what constituted a heap of coffee on a teaspoon. It'd dawned on Karen that's all Patricia saw of her potential – a glorified maid.

With Karen being a newly qualified accountant, she posted her CV on the internet that night.

Patricia was mid-fifties, with a shock of grey hair. She spoke with a well-educated tongue and openly looked down on Karen with obvious contempt.

Karen pulled the soggy handkerchief from under the sleeve of her lilac jumper and wiped her runny nose, whilst stifling the sneeze that'd been tickling her nose since Patricia had commenced her latest rant.

Her head cold made her feel terrible, the Sudafed she had dry swallowed earlier had yet to work its magic against the hot vice that gripped her head.

Unsubtle detestation was written over Patricia's stuffy face.

The final straw came when Patricia covered her nose and mouth with her right manicured hand and instructed Karen to put the kettle on.

She automatically flicked the switch on the green kettle and lifted three mugs from the drain board that she'd polished earlier. Through her fits of coughing, Karen managed to have the perfect heap of coffee into Patricia's Kermit the Frog mug. It was at this moment, staring at the grinning Kermit that Karen decided to hand in her notice.

Relief washed over her. It was the correct decision. She'd come into work feeling unwell and had been subjected to making coffee, sweeping floors and polishing desks. This was not what she'd spent all those years at university for.

She didn't mean to sneeze into Patricia's coffee. Her first thought was to pour it out and remake it, but somehow couldn't find the motivation. She wiped her nose with her handkerchief and took the coffee to her boss.

Karen didn't have the stomach to watch her creation devoured. She handed Patricia and Betty their coffees before picking up her handbag. Then she left for lunch; never to return.

The next morning, Karen telephoned the office.

"Hi Betty, its Karen. Can I speak to Patricia, please?"

"Patricia isn't in today – she is off sick…With the flu."

About the author

Claire Wilson is an aspiring crime writer from Falkirk, Scotland. When she is not editing her crime series to death, she likes to dabble in shorter fiction. Her work has been published in several anthologies and she is seeking representation. You can follow Claire's progress on Twitter.com/byclairewilson

Greener Pastures was awarded joint 5th place in the competition.

The Carrot Fly Machine *by Alan R Paine*

Laila was glad to change out of the clothes she'd been wearing in the lab all afternoon and put on shorts and a light cotton top. Even she was impressed by how good she looked and she set off to try and find Simon. He wasn't answering his messages but this was no surprise.

She found him surrounded by an array of gadgets, next to the Agricultural Department's experimental vegetable plot.

'Whatever are you doing here? I was wondering where you'd got to.'

'It's my final year project,' he said only giving her the briefest of glances. 'This drone is controlled by the laptop. It's an electronic simulation of a carrot fly.'

'A what?'

'A carrot fly. It's an insect that lays its eggs in carrots. These sensors can detect the substances that give carrots their unique smell. The computer is running a program emulating exactly how the fly's brain works so the drone will fly around the garden and descend onto the carrot patch ignoring all other vegetables.'

'What do the Aggies think about this?'

'Don't tell them. Why do you think I'm here after hours?'

'How big is a carrot fly?' said Laila.

'Five millimetres or so,' said Simon.

'So, its brain must be tiny.'

'About the size of a pinhead.'

Laila looked doubtful. 'And you need all this lot to do the same thing?'

'This is ground breaking research. One day we'll be able to emulate a human mind in a space no bigger than someone's head.'

'Sounds scary,' said Laila. 'Let's see what robo-fly can do.'

Laila watched as the drone zig-zagged across the garden with no apparent purpose before landing in the middle of some young lettuces. Simon swore. He stared at the laptop screen, scrolling through endless lines of letters and numbers. It was no use talking to him now, she thought. What would she have to do to get him to take any notice of her? She wondered if dressing like a carrot would do the trick but then thought better of it and quietly walked away.

About the author

Stories by Alan R Paine have been published in five Fantastic Books competition collections: *Dread Cold*, *Dreaming of Steam*, *The Forge*, *The Dummies Guide to Serial Killing*, and now *Kaleidoscope*. His story 'Trains of Thought' in *Dreaming of Steam*, won the Julia Bradbury prize for capturing the spirit of the Wolds.

He collaborated with Drew Wagar and seven other writers to produce the science fiction anthology 'Nine Streams of Consciousness,' and he has published the short novel 'Faraway Sky, Ocean Deep' which was written, from beginning to end, in the month of November 2020 in response to the challenge set by nanowrimo.org.

Alan's debut full-length Sci-Fi novel, A Suggestion in Space, was launched at the same time as this anthology.

Alan enjoys amateur theatre and has written and directed short plays and sketches including a play performed on line during lockdown.

The Carrot Fly was shortlisted in the competition.

Dragon Ninja *by Jack Mann*

Ninjas flew across the sky, felling dragons.

"Kenshirou! A second wave approaches from the east!"

"Understood," muttered Kenshirou, drawing his dragon blade; a wide katana made of diamond-steel. Pivoting upon a cloud, he turned and leapt towards the winged monsters bearing down on them. "Naruto, Kenshin, Musashi, with me!"

Three other ninjas joined him.

"There are so many. Will the four of us be enough?" asked Kenshin.

Kenshirou spat, but unfortunately he was wearing a mask, so this just made his face wet. "Let cowardly thoughts not taint the purity of your souls."

"Yes my lord!" cried Kenshin.

The dragons grew near. Five came ahead of the main group, their talons ready, flames rising from their nostrils.

"When the wind shifts in your direction, you've got to catch it and fly with it like it's your last breath!" cried Kenshirou.

"The wind is our guide, our energy, our weapon," responded the others in unison.

Kenshirou planted his foot upon a focus of dense air in the sky, a narrowing of chakra that, to a ninja, provided enough energy from which to jump, and propelled himself forward. He swung his dragon-blade and cleaved the nearest dragon's head in two. His comrades joined him, decapitating, de-winging, and slitting the throats of the other four.

As the vast, lifeless bodies dropped to the earth below, the rest of the horde before them gathered into a formation.

"Halt!" cried Kenshirou. He channelled chakra into the air below his feet to remain aloft. "Fireball-of-ultimate-death jitsu!"

His three companions formed up around him, so that they presented a diamond to the onrushing horde. They raised their hands, brought them in front of themselves, made tortured-snake stance, and then clapped three times. A huge ball of glowing energy appeared before them. Kenshirou head-butted it, hurling it towards the dragons.

The dragon horde from the East tried to break away in panic, but the energy collided with them, obliterating each creature into tiny shards of scale and bone.

"Excellent," said Kenshirou.

"We have defeated this attack," said Naruto, "but our energies are nearly spent."

"Let us flank the horde engaging our friends and destroy them in hand-to-hand combat," said Kenshirou.

"Affirmative!" chorused the other three ninjas.

They leapt towards where the main battle still raged, but Kenshirou saw something. "What is that?"

Hovering below the warring dragons and ninjas was a cowled figure in purple robes, reading from a wooden tablet.

"It is an evil lord!" cried Musashi.

"I thought they were all imprisoned!" cried Kenshin.

"That fool Yamamoto must have released one to harness their powers against the dragons," said Kenshirou. He almost spat again, but remembered this was a bad idea.

Just then the tablet exploded, and purple fire shot from the evil lord's hands. With it he scorched the dragons and the ninjas, turning all in the battle to cinders.

"Nooooo!!!!" cried Naruto.

"Avenge our comrades!" cried Kenshirou. "Mete out death in our fury, and meet our own deaths with honour!"

About the author

Jack Mann, a Medical Doctor working in the UK, had been nursing an ambition to write a science fiction novel since primary school. A series of books is in the works, set in a future where technological advances have left us less, rather than more, dependent on artificial intelligence. His debut novel, *Gravity's Arrow*, and his short story, *The Sufferers* (published in our 666 horror anthology) are already in print. This work of flash fiction, inspired by a childhood fascination with samurais, ninjas and monsters, takes tropes to the extreme in a clash of thrills, comedy and action.

Dragon Ninja was shortlisted in the competition.

Anyone's Rift *by Annie Percik*

The air in front of Alistair rippled, warping and twisting in an obscene way that reminded him of frogspawn. The resulting membrane split open, letting out a rush of air that was considerably warmer than the chill London night around him. He took an involuntary step backwards, as the tear in the fabric of reality widened, showing a void beyond, filled with swirling colours, like a psychedelic aurora.

It had worked. He couldn't believe the ritual had actually worked. Now he would be able to show those arrogant bastards at the Artisans of Wizarding Guild that he was worthy of membership. And if he could engineer a portal to another realm, anybody could. Those snooty wizards would have to relax their eligibility requirements now.

Alistair edged forwards again, inching towards the rift in the air before him. What might await him on the other side? The very air itself might imbue him with untold new abilities, which could raise his wizarding skills to a whole new level. He reached out one hand towards the gap, marvelling at the way the coloured light played over his fingers.

Just as he was about to breach the threshold, a tentacle shot out and wrapped itself around his wrist. Its suckers stuck fast to his skin with incredible strength and it started pulling him towards the opening. He leaned back with all his body weight, but he was helpless against the power of the creature that now had him firmly within its grasp.

As Alistair opened his mouth to scream, the tentacle

yanked him through the portal, and the tear in reality closed up neatly behind him, leaving only the echo of sinister laughter on the last of the balmy breeze.

About the author

Annie Percik lives in London, writing novels and short stories, whilst working as a freelance editor. She writes a blog about writing on her website, which is where all her current publications are listed, including her novels, *The Defiant Spark* and *A Spectrum of Heroes*. She hosts a media review podcast and publishes a photo-story blog, recording the adventures of her teddy bear. He is much more popular online than she is. See https://alobear.co.uk for more information.

Anyone's Rift was awarded joint 3rd place in the competition.

A Gift From The Sky *by John Kot*

The fireball streaking across the sky stirred the old man from his fitful sleep, and then the impact shook him fully awake, rattling the wood and paper screen doors of his bedroom. He reached for his glasses, then climbed stiffly from the *futon* and shuffled barefoot across the *tatami* floor. Pausing to slip his old *geta* onto his feet, he made his way outside. Silence. Had it been a dream? But there was a metallic smell in the night air, and he could make out an unfamiliar shadow in the rice field. He hurried past the stone channel that carried the spring meltwater from the mountain, past the sleeping carp in their pond, and discovered a mound of fresh dirt, with a wisp of vapour rising into the night sky. Some solid object had fallen from the vast emptiness above him, like a gift from the cold, silent stars, and buried itself in the earth. For a moment it seemed incomprehensible; and then he was down on his knees, digging like one of the badgers in the forest until his arthritic fingers struck the hard iron mass.

At first light, he carried it, wrapped in a piece of sackcloth, out to the forge: cold and disused, but ready. Taking his old knife – the one he used in the kitchen these days to slice the *daikon* of which he had grown so fond – he deftly split a piece of seasoned bamboo, shaving the wood with the razor-sharp blade to make a handful of kindling. Then, cutting a notch, he sawed one piece of bamboo against the other until a wisp of smoke appeared. Blowing softly, he held the kindling against the glowing ember and, when it caught, carried it across to the cold brick hearth, cradling the tiny flame in his hands. Using small sticks, then charcoal, ignoring the ache in his shoulder as he pumped the wooden handle of the bellows, he built the fire until he had a mound of glowing coals, with small blue flames chasing across the surface. Carefully, reverently, he took the sky stone and placed it into the heart of the fire, where it nestled like a black egg.

A lifetime's work flashed before him: the flawless blades; the blades that had cracked and warped; the triumphs and the disappointments. For the first time, he understood that they had all been just a rehearsal for this one final task: to reveal the perfect blade hidden within this piece of a fallen star. Gripping the glowing orb with pincers, he transferred it carefully to the anvil. As he wiped the beads of sweat from his brow, he suddenly thought of sweet *Yui-chan*, before the hateful illness had taken her, and found his eyes were watering.

'Old chimney needs sweeping,' he muttered to himself.

He felt the weight of the hammer, its familiar wooden handle warm and smooth against his scarred hand. What do you do when the iron's hot? Ah yes, you should strike.

About the author

John Kot grew up in Sheffield, England. As a young child, he was obsessed with space exploration and the Apollo Moon landings. This enthusiasm led him to a career in science and engineering, completing his PhD at the University of Bath. In 1988, he moved to Australia to take a "temporary" job with an Australian government research laboratory, but met a Canadian girl, Jeanne, who was studying for her PhD at a Sydney university, and who shared his love of science, the ocean, and scuba diving. They eventually married and settled in Sydney's Northern Beaches, where they still live. They have two children, now grown up, who also live and work in Sydney.

A Gift from the Sky came joint 4th in the competition.

Between *by Erin Warden English*

Inspector Fox squinted down at the photograph, discerning its contents despite the reflection of the bright Italian sun. A man lay, face towards the camera, in a lavishly ornate Catholic church. Blood seeped from a wound in his head, into a puddle on the tiled floor.

He grunted, handing the photograph back to Inspector Williams.

"And you're the lucky sod who gets to follow up the case in Rome," he said.

"Not so lucky," Williams replied unhappily. "The man is Daniel Long. Head of a big textiles company thinking about relocating from England to Italy. Lots of people very unhappy about that. He was reported missing in Florence a week ago by his wife. Yesterday we're sent this photo – anonymously. Seems Long has been murdered – but the question is, where?"

"Seems simple enough," said Fox. "Have you identified the church?"

"That's the problem," Williams continued as they strolled along the Tiber. "Nobody can identify it. Some expert pinpointed it as Rome, based on the architecture, but the place is littered with churches – there's hundreds. And not one of those churches has reported having found a dead body in it – that's the really bizarre thing."

"You've asked the Catholics?"

"Of course. Not one priest or friar will claim the church as his. The parishioners seem just as clueless."

"A disused church then?"

"Not likely – look, in the picture there are fresh flowers. But we checked them. Twenty-seven in total on record, and none looking like this."

They walked in silence for a bit.

"You're absolutely sure?" asked Fox. "Nobody recognised it at all?"

"There was one false alarm," Williams confessed. "An old man seemed certain. Kept saying it was 'between the churches at Sant-Angelo and Umberto'. But we checked, and there was no church there at all."

Fox snapped his head up suddenly.

"Tell me about your translator," he said quickly. "I assume they gave you one?"

"They did," Williams replied. "A young kid, straight out of university. Seemed nervous. Kept checking words in his little dictionary. But he was sure of those names – there was no mistaking the names."

"No mistaking the names perhaps," Fox said, picking up his pace. "But something else may have got lost in translation."

Williams looked at him, puzzled.

"Look again at the flowers – red on the left, white on the right. The man said the picture was of a church between the churches at Sant-Angelo and Umberto. He meant a *cross* between. The photo – it's an edit."

"But why–?"

"Why would someone send you a picture of a dead body and fail to report it? Whoever sent you this is trying to divert the police investigation. I would bet you anything – Daniel Long, dead or alive, is still in Florence. You've been on a wild goose chase round Rome, looking for a church that *doesn't exist."*

"Then – in Florence, when we were sniffing around–?"

"You were probably on the right track," Fox said grimly. "I'd hurry back, if I were you."

About the author

Erin Warden-English is a PhD researcher in Visual Neuroscience. She loves to read and write murder mysteries, and is particularly inspired by Agatha Christie, Arthur Conan-Doyle, and Henry James. She lives in Leeds with her husband and three pet rats.

Between was shortlisted in the competition.

The Last Word *by Kester Robert Park*

'What is a book to you? Something you fall into, plummet and come up soaring? Well, that's very sweet. I wish my books could be such confectionery. My books are woven with the First Word, the one that created this world. They are even more powerful than I am, just as they ought.

'As a Witch of the Source, I am charged with enforcing the iron-cast rules of the universe, quite a task when you consider–'

A creak like a door opening reaches me from high up in the deep-blueing forest air.

'Oh, they are not supposed to do that. What is the punishment for coming into the forest after official visiting hours, passing in through the music of bending trees? My books will know. They will tell me.'

Cries issue now, from a constellation of points drawn in a tangle around my abode.

'Well, at least I needn't go looking for them.'

The door of the hut explodes, bouncing off the inside wall. There, in the doorway, is a hunched, naked, wiry being, head lowered, eyes raised, red coursing from a pair of hands each clenching a sliver of metal. Then, another behind it. I can see it is frustrated to be second in line, yet relieved not to be first. Its mind is a light just bright enough to cast out the darkness of unconsciousness, not bright enough to resolve its own internal contradictions.

'This is why I'm so busy.'

Half a dozen of them squeeze into the shack, which you can now see is a short scream from the boggy mulch of the forest floor. They throng me. An arm with a flap of skin drooping from an infected wound punches through the maze of limbs, beards and torsos to knock the hat from my head. One of them drools, giggles and sets itself to cutting locks of silver from my head. When they are finished undressing and shaving me, they cut off my fingers and toes.

I sing a song of pain, and I go up in my voice and live in the air while my body is undone, my intestines spooled out and passed around and ingested. When my voice comes back to the world like a feather, my body is gone. My books are gone: my Books of Punishment. My home is scorched, and the tree in which it was seated is aflame.

The creatures have run away with my material fragments and, now, with sight which issues from a drift of steam, I see they have scampered into the forest to burn them, my books and my remains, chanting in their primitive dialect, 'The witch can't hurt us, anymore,' around the flames.

They think, in destroying my body, they have killed me. They haven't killed me. They've released me. They think, in destroying my books, they have destroyed my power. They don't understand. I used the books not to empower, but to restrain myself.

About the author

Kester Robert Park is from Scotland and lives in Quito, Ecuador, with his wife and daughter. This is his eighth short story published by Fantastic Books Publishing across four anthologies, including *Dread Cold*, *The Dummies Guide to Serial Killing* and *666*.

You can follow, and be followed by, Kester at twitter.com/tinklebadger and read stories, essays and poems in English and Spanish at tenderlemonstration.wordpress.com.

The Last Word was awarded joint 5th place in the competition.

The Camera Never Lies *by Ian Coldicott*

The woman let herself into Martin's house. She still had the front door key he lent her when they were lovers. She hadn't meant to keep it. But Martin was blackmailing her. She remembered the camera that he'd bought for his photography evening class – he'd used it to take sexually explicit photographs of her. At the time, she went along with the idea. She found him strangely attractive. Now he was threatening to send the pictures to her husband unless she paid him what was an extortionate amount of money. No way was she going along with that! He hadn't been all that good in bed, anyway.

She knew he would be out at his evening class. It would be the perfect time to search for the embarrassing photographs. She began in the living room. There was a bookcase and a sideboard. Nothing doing. Just bills, receipts, some cheap paperbacks, old love letters, and some car magazines. She became increasingly frustrated. Nowhere obvious to store photographs, no locked drawers, no rolls of film. Suddenly she lost patience and swept the contents of a bookshelf onto the floor. She shouted obscenities, pushing over a table and chairs.

Upstairs, she went into the main bedroom. It brought back unsettling memories. She couldn't face doing more than a cursory search. She tried the back bedroom and pulled some files off a bookcase, flicking through each one hurriedly before moving on to the next. She knocked a picture off the wall, swearing loudly. She cursed Martin –

where could he have hidden those photographs? Then suddenly she found what she was looking for. A nondescript plain brown envelope lying on a shelf. Inside, the photographs and negatives. Everything seemed to be there. 'Martin, you bastard!', she shouted. Then she went into the bathroom, intending to flush it all down the lavatory. But she slipped and fell forwards, hitting her head heavily on the side of the washbasin. Everything went black. The photographic evidence, discovered so successfully, lay scattered beside her body.

Not long afterwards, Martin returned home. His class had finished early. He looked with disbelief at the scene of devastation downstairs. He thought he should call the police. A few minutes later was surprised to see and hear a police car pull up outside, blue lights flashing. He opened the door to a tall, intimidating police officer and his shorter colleague.

'Where is she, Mr Jones?' the tall one demanded. 'Your neighbour made a 999 call saying she heard a woman screaming and shouting your name, and the sound of furniture being pushed over. We're very concerned for her safety. We've had our eye on you for some time.'

'What woman?'

'You know who I mean.'

The shorter officer went to look upstairs. When she came down, she looked distraught.

'She's in the bathroom. She's dead.'

The woman was found with a severe head injury, lying next to a heap of photographs. Things didn't look good for Martin. The camera never lies.

About the author

Ian Coldicott has been writing short and micro-fiction and poetry for a couple of years. He has enjoyed some moderate success, reaching several long lists and short lists, having submissions published, and being placed in a couple of competitions. He lives in Lichfield, Staffordshire.

The Camera Never Lies was joint runner-up in the competition.

About the Competition and the Charity Anthologies

Kaleidoscope is our 10th charity anthology and our first based on a flash fiction competition.

Instead of a conventional entry fee, writers were asked to make a donation to one of two charities: *Special Effect* or *Stack Up*. Their donation receipt was their ticket to enter. We did not require disclosure of the amount paid, so can't be precise as to how much was raised but we estimate the average donation to have been higher than a conventional entry fee for such a competition. In the end, three separate charities benefitted because one entrant misread the rules and donated to a different organisation. It was a generous donation and all in a good cause so we turned a blind eye to this breach of the rules.

Entrants chose from a list of quotations and wrote their pieces around their chosen quote. For a full list of the choices they were given, go to the competition page on our website. The following are the quotations chosen by the authors of the shortlisted entries published in Kaleidoscope. Some authors chose to quote the extracts word for word within their stories, some took the essence of the quotation and built their pieces around it. We hope you will agree that they all made effective use of the excerpt they chose.

- Every now and again a 12-year-old boy wanders along our carriage in both directions, the frequency and intervals of his passing suggesting that he's amusing

himself walking from one end of this enormous train to the other and then all the way back again.
From Fragments of Joy and Sorrow *by Alan Wakeman*

- "When the wind shifts in your direction, you've got to catch it and fly with it like it's your last breath!"
From The Purple Bowtie by Lisabeth Reynolds

- Early attempts at colonising Mars were clean, as no native population was displaced, but they weren't straightforward.
From Generation Mars: book 1 Blood Red Dust by Stuart Aken

- His engineer mind itched to find out what was going on and his social conscience couldn't dismiss the potential ramifications.
From The Defiant Spark by Annie Percik

- I shall move from this world to the next like a petal blown on the winds of dreams.
From Tesserae by BJ Edwards

- It's all about you: motivation and time.
From My Dalek has a Puncture by Simon Fisher Becker

- Nestled unobtrusively in the maze of tiny back streets between the bridges Ponte Sant'Angelo and Ponte Umberto 1, was the most unrecognisable church in Rome.
From The Triple Goddess by Michael James

- She licked her lips. It had been satisfying, but the burning embers of vengeance were still smouldering within her.
From the Shadeward series by Drew Wagar

- Sitting in the garden as the sun goes down.
From Faith by Christian Danvers

- "What do you do when the iron's hot? Ah yes, you should strike."

Fantastic Books Charity Anthologies

The Dummies' Guide to Serial Killing – an eclectic collection to celebrate female strength that donates to the Global Fund for Women. Winner of the Crime Writers' Association Short Story Dagger.

Dread Cold – a horror collection that donates to Anti-slavery International and Embrace the Middle East.

The Forge – a Sci-Fan collection that donates to Fibromyalgia Action UK.

Synthesis – a science fiction and fantasy collection that donates to Freedom from Torture.

Fusion – a science fiction and fantasy collection that donates to the World Cancer Research Fund.

666 – a horror collection of stories of exactly 666 words that donates to EDS-UK.

aMUSEing Tales – a collection of children's stories that donates to the WorldWide Orphans Foundation.

Ours – an international poetry collection that donates to the WorldWide Orphans Foundation.

Dreaming of Steam – 23 tales of Wolds and rails that donates to the Yorkshire Wolds Railway.

You can find more delightful tales and wonderfully woven prose at our Fantastic Books Store.

www.fantasticbooksstore.com

www.ingramcontent.com/pod-product-compliance
Lightning Source LLC
Chambersburg PA
CBHW060236180626
46813CB00007B/3115